Contents

© Brimax Books Ltd 1988.

Published by Longmeadow Press, 201 High Ridge Road, Stamford,
CT 06904. All rights reserved. No part of this book may be
reproduced or utilized in any form or by any means,
electronic or mechanical, including photocopying, recording
or by any information storage and retrieval system, without
permission in writing from the Publisher.

Library of Congress Cataloging-in-Publication Data
ISBN: 0-681-45436-9
Printed in Dubai
First Longmeadow Press Edition
0 9 8 7 6 5 4 3 2 1

STORIES TO READ BY MYSELF

Written and illustrated by Sue Camm

LONGMEADOW
P R E S S

Tinka Elephant's Nose

Tinka the baby elephant
lives in Africa.
It is very hot there, but
Tinka's home is in a cool
and shady forest.
Tinka has a very long nose.
It is called a trunk.
All elephants have trunks.
Tinka likes to play
in the forest.

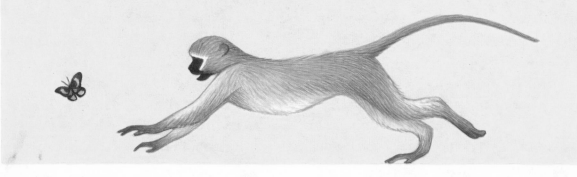

Mick Monkey makes fun
of Tinka Elephant.
"You do look funny!
My nose is neat and flat,
so I do not bump it when
I climb the trees," he says.
Mick jumps onto a branch
and swings by his tail.
"Maybe my nose is too
long," says Tinka.

Poll Parrot makes fun
of Tinka Elephant.
"You do look funny! I have
a hard beak. I can crack
nuts open with my beak,"
says Poll Parrot.
Then, Poll spreads her
wings and flies away.
"I am sure my nose is too
long," says Tinka.

Little Wild Pig makes fun
of Tinka Elephant.
"You do look funny! My
nose is short and strong.
I can dig up nice roots
to eat. Look, like this."
He digs with his nose in
the soft ground.
"Now I know my nose is
too long!" says Tinka.

Tiny Giraffe makes fun
of Tinka Elephant.
"You do look funny! I have
a short black nose. Your
nose is so long it must
get in the way when you
run!" says Tiny Giraffe.
Then, he flicks his tail
and runs into the forest.
"I wish I had a short nose
like Tiny," says
Tinka Elephant.

"The animals make fun of my long nose," says Tinka to her mother. "Can I make my trunk grow short?"
"You are silly," says her mother. "A long nose is a great help to an elephant. Just wait and see!
Now go and play so I can have a sleep."

Tinka plays by the river.
Mick Monkey is on the
other side of the river.
"How can I cross over?" he
says. "I cannot swim!"
"Wait, I can help you,"
says Tinka.
See how she helps Mick to
cross the river.
"I am sorry I made fun of
your nose. It is
a great help!"

Who is this in the river?
Splash! Splash!
"Help!" says Poll Parrot.
"Get me out of the water!"
See how Tinka pulls her out.
"Thank you," says Poll.
"I fell in when I was
washing my tail. Your trunk
has saved me. I am glad
that you have a long nose!"

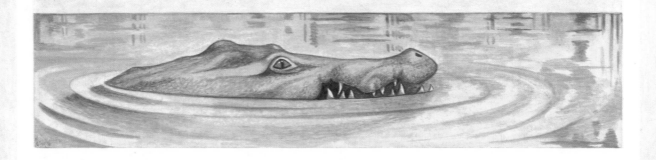

Tinka and her new friends
meet Little Wild Pig as
he digs up some roots.
"The best root goes under
this heavy log. I cannot
dig it up," he says.
Tinka can help. See how
she moves the heavy log.
"I will not make fun of
your nose again," says
Little Wild Pig
as he runs away.

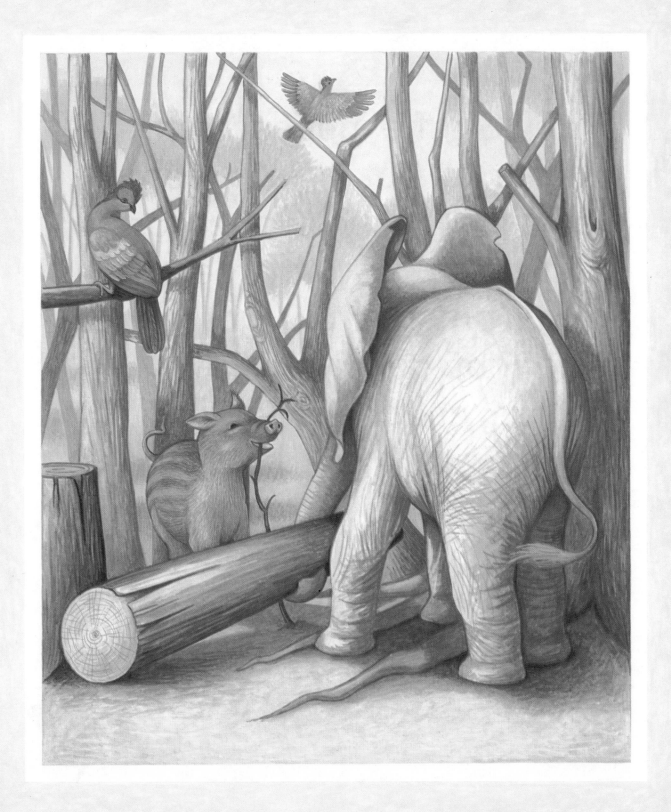

Tiny Giraffe needs help.
"I like to eat new green
leaves. The best ones are
at the top of the tree.
But I am not big yet and
I cannot get them."
"I can get them for you,"
says Tinka. See how she
picks the new green leaves.
"A long nose can be a
great help after
all!" says Tinka.

Tinka sniffs the air.
"What a funny smell!"
she says.
Poll Parrot can see a long
way. "Smoke!" she says.
"There is a fire in the forest.
What can we do?"
Tinka knows what to do.
She puts her trunk in the
air. She calls to all the
elephants in
the forest.

Mother Elephant and all
the big elephants come
to help.
"We must get water to put
out the fire!" says Tinka.
The elephants go to the
river and they suck lots
of water into their trunks.
See how they put out
the fire.

The fire is out and the forest is safe again.
"Hurray!" say Mick Monkey and Poll Parrot.
"Hurray!" say Little Wild Pig and Tiny Giraffe.
"Three cheers for all the elephants!" they say.
"Three cheers for Tinka the Elephant's nose!"

Say these words again

elephant	giraffe
monkey	parrot
shady	flicks
climb	swings
branch	crack
leaves	hurray
cheers	splash
spreads	heavy
friends	washing
other	mother

How does Tinka help her friends?

Ben Bear's Pot of Gold

Ben, the little brown bear, wants to go out to play. "You cannot go out in the rain," says Mother Bear. She looks to see if the clouds have gone away. "Ben!" she says. "Look at the rainbow in the sky." The rainbow goes all the way to the Misty Hills. It ends at a tall pine tree.

"There is a story about a rainbow," says Mother Bear. "At the end of a rainbow there is a pot of gold." "Our rainbow ends at the tall pine tree," says Ben. "What fun! I can go to look for gold in the Misty Hills. I can look for it by the tall pine tree."

Ben sets off with a picnic box. It is full of good things to eat.

"Hello! Are you going to have a picnic?" says Bob the beaver.

"No," says Ben. "I am off to the Misty Hills. I want to find the pot of gold at the end of the rainbow."

"I will come too!" says Bob.

Ben and Bob set off down
the path. They meet
Skipper the chipmunk.
"We are on our way to the
Misty Hills," says Ben.
"There is a pot of gold
at the end of the rainbow.
We are going to find it,
by the tall pine tree."
"What fun!" says Skipper.
"Wait for me,
I will come too!"

Ben, Bob and Skipper
follow the path to the
Misty Hills.
"We are off to look for
gold by the tall pine
tree," sings Ben.
"We will find the pot
of gold," sings Bob.
Meg the magpie hears them.
"What fun!" she says.

"Wait for me,
I will come too!"

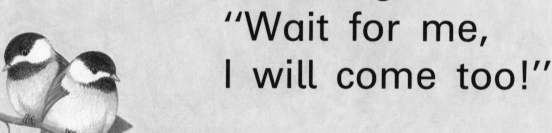

It is a very long way
to the Misty Hills.
They stop at a pond to
drink. Bob the beaver
has a swim.
"This is a lovely pond to
swim in," he says.
"Swimming is what I like
to do best of all."
"We can call it Bob's Pond,"
says Ben. "But
now we must go."

They have a long way to go
so they rest in the forest.
Skipper finds an old log.
"This would make a lovely
house," he says.
"The best kind of house
for a chipmunk is inside
an old log."
"We can call it Skipper's
Log," says Ben.
"But now we
must go on."

They all go along the path
to the Misty Hills.
"Where is Meg the magpie?"
"Here I am," says Meg.
"Look what I have found.
Red berries! I do love
red berries."
She eats until she is full.
"We can call this Meg's
Berry Place," says Ben.
                    "But now we
                    must go on."

Skipper, Bob and Meg
go along the path
to the Misty Hills.
Is Ben lost?
No, here he is with a
very sticky face!
"I have found a bees' nest
full of honey," he says.
"We can call it Ben's Honey
Place," says Bob.
"But now we
must go on."

The path goes up a hill.
The ground is hard and
full of rocks and stones.
"We are in the Misty Hills,"
says Ben. "There is the tall
pine tree. That is where
I saw the rainbow end.
That is where we have
to go to find the pot
of gold."

They go to the tall pine
tree and look for the
pot of gold.
"There is nothing up here,"
says Meg the magpie.
"Nothing down here,"
says Bob the beaver.
"Nothing here at all!"
says Skipper sadly.
Ben is sad too, but he
says, "Never
mind the gold . . .

. . . Bob has found a lovely
pond to swim in.
Skipper has found a new
log house to live in.
Meg has found lots of nice
berries to eat.
I have found a store full
of sweet honey.
We have all found our own
pot of gold!"

They are all very happy.
They make a camp fire and
sit round it. They eat the
food from the picnic box.
"It is a long way home,"
says Ben, "but it was fun
to go to the end of the
rainbow!"
Do you think there is a
pot of gold at the end of
the rainbow?
Maybe there is.

Say these words again

little	brown
Mother	clouds
rainbow	story
picnic	things
beaver	chipmunk
wait	follow
magpie	swimming
lovely	sticky
where	nothing
misty	Hello

What are they doing?

Mandy Mouse's Birthday

Mandy Mouse looks out
of her front door. The sun
is shining in a blue sky.
"What a lovely day for my
birthday," says Mandy.
"I think I will go and
see Silky Squirrel. I can
tell her it is my birthday
and maybe she will come
out to play. We can play
hide and seek
in the trees."

Mandy goes to look for her
friend Silky. She runs to
the forest. She finds the
tree where Silky lives.
Here is Silky Squirrel at
the bottom of the tree.
"Hello Silky," says Mandy.
"Do you know what day it
is? It is my birthday, and
the sun is shining, so
will you come
out to play?"

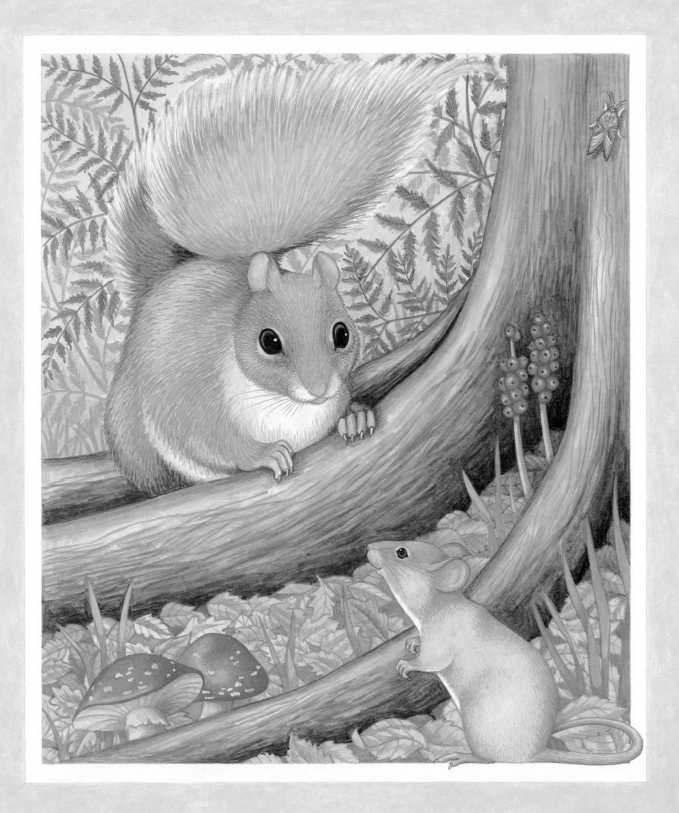

"Oh, I am sorry Mandy,"
says Silky. "Today I will
be too busy. My food store
is nearly empty. I must go
and find some more nuts to
fill it up."
Poor little Mandy!
"Never mind," she says.
"I will go and see Ricky
Rabbit. He will come and
play hopping
races with me!"

Mandy goes to look for her friend Ricky. She finds the path that leads out of the forest, into the field where Ricky lives.
Here is Ricky, hopping along the forest path.
"Hello Ricky!" says Mandy. "Do you know it is my birthday? Will you come and play hopping races with me?"

"Dear me, Mandy," says Ricky. "I have too much work to do. I must sweep out my house and find some clean dry leaves to put on the floor. I have no time to play with you today!"
Poor little Mandy!
"Never mind," she says. "Fred Frog will play boats with me. I will go to the pond."

Mandy goes to look for her friend Fred. She pushes between the flowers and grass in the field, to the damp, mossy side of the pond. Here is Fred Frog, sitting on a lily leaf. "Hello Fred," says Mandy. "Will you come and play boats with me? We can use the lily flowers for our boats."

Fred Frog is very sorry.
"I am far too busy," he says.
"I have to show all the
little frogs how to dive.
I have no time to play
games with you!"
"But it is my birthday,"
says Mandy, "and I want to
have some fun. Why are all
my friends so busy today?"

Poor little Mandy. Fred jumps into the pond and swims away. Mandy feels sad all by herself.

"Silky has to find some nuts," she says.

"Ricky has to sweep his house. Fred must teach the little frogs to dive. If there is no one to play with, I may as well go home."

On her way home, Mandy
sees Rob Robin fly past.
Rob Robin is the little
bird that brings all the
letters for the animals.
Mandy can see a letter
in his beak.
"I wonder who that letter
is for?" says Mandy Mouse.
"I hope it is for me!"

The letter is for Mandy!
Rob Robin has left it on
the doorstep. Mandy reads
the name on the outside.
It says, "TO MISS MOUSE."
"Yes!" says Mandy.
"There is no mistake.
The letter is for me!"
She opens it and reads,
"Dear Mandy, will you
come to the old
house today?"

"How funny!" says Mandy. "Who is it from? No one lives in the old house any more. Is it a joke? I must go and find out!"

She runs down the lane to the house. Roses grow all over the walls and cobwebs hang at the windows. The house looks empty. The door is open and Mandy peeps in . . .

"Happy birthday Mandy!
This is a party for you,"
says Silky Squirrel.
"It is hard to keep a
secret and not give the
game away!" says Ricky.
"Do you like your presents
too?" says Fred.
Mandy opens her presents.
There is a nutshell cup,
a leafy hat and
a water lily boat!

They play hide and seek in the dark corners of the old house. They hop and race up and down the path outside the house.

They play in the lily boat. When they are hungry there is birthday cake to eat.

"Thank you!" says Mandy. "My birthday has been fun!"

Say these words again

shining	squirrel
birthday	friend
bottom	busy
corners	hopping
sweep	leaves
pushes	flowers
mossy	sorry
herself	animals
wonder	doorstep
mistake	empty